AF615129

# SEA CREATURES

## A Colors of Nature Book

Written by Malcolm Whyte
Illustrated by Andrea Tachiera

**TROUBADOR PRESS**
*a subsidiary of*
PRICE STERN SLOAN

Copyright © 1989 by Word Play, Inc. and Andrea Tachiera
Published by Price Stern Sloan, Inc., 360 North La Cienega Boulevard, Los Angeles, California 90048
Printed in the United States of America. All rights reserved. No part of this publication may be reproduced, stored in a retrieval system or transmitted, in any form or by any means, electronic, mechanical, photocopying, recording or otherwise, without the prior written permission of the publishers.
ISBN: 0-8431-1959-4 10 9 8 7 6 5 4 3 2 1

# BLUE FIN TUNA

## *Thunnus thynnus*

*Range: worldwide* *Length: 14 feet (4.2 m)*

The oceans were formed about 500 million years ago. Below the sea water that covers 71% of the earth's surface, the ocean plunges to depths of six miles (10 km). Between the surface and the floor swims a parade of fantastic sea life, from tiny, one-celled protozoa to the mighty whales. Here big fish eat little fish, and little fish eat smaller fish; every species needs some defense. The blue fin tuna's defense is to form a "school" by swimming together in a large group. It's much more difficult for a predator to attack a crowd than a lone fish. Size helps the blue fin, too, as they can grow to weigh 1800 pounds (818 kg)!

These open ocean fish are just a small part of the immense resources contained in the sea, which teems with minerals, plants and other animals. Protecting these resources and keeping the oceans clean is vital to their survival, and of great benefit to mankind.

# KILLER WHALE

## *Orcinus orca*

*Range: worldwide* *Length: 28 feet (8.5 m)*

Some sixty million years ago a species of mammal left solid ground to return to the sea for food and protection. These animals evolved into whales and dolphins. The killer whale is the largest member of the dolphin family. Orcas, as they are also called, are striking, black-and-white sea mammals whose curiosity and intelligence make them the top attraction at sea life parks. The tricks they do—jumping, racing, standing up, slapping the water—are all natural behaviors of the orcas that the park trainers work into the act.

Although there is no record of human death due to killer whales, they are deadly predators of other large sea creatures. Swimming in packs, their slashing cone-shaped teeth seek porpoises, penguins, seals and sea lions, as well as fish and squid. They've even been known to attack the giant 100-foot-long (30.3-m) blue whale, thereby earning their name.

# AMERICAN LOBSTER

## *Homarus americanus*

*Range: Atlantic coast    Length: 24 inches (61 cm)*

Lobsters belong to a class of animals called *Crustacea* which includes crayfish, crabs and shrimp. Their skeleton is made up of jointed parts which they shed as they grow. An adult lobster, such as the American lobster, weighs from twenty-five to thirty pounds (11 to 13.6 kg). After laying up to 50,000 eggs, the female gathers them up and carries them under her abdomen for eleven months, at the end of which they will hatch. The babies then float near the water's surface to feed on plankton (microscopic plant and animal life).

The American lobster has a greenish-brown protective coloring. It swims very fast—backward—by rapidly flexing its broad tail under it. Hiding under rocks and ledges in tide pools, it claws at passing food and scoops it into its mouth. Besides marine insects, worms, small crustaceans and fish, lobsters also eat dead animal matter, thereby helping to keep the ocean waters clean.

# SWORDFISH

## *Xiphius gladius*

*Range: warm tropical seas worldwide* *Length: 18 feet (5.5 m)*

A swordfish slips below the rolling green water along the Florida coast, its tall dorsal (back) fin slicing the surface. Behind, a stiff, half-moon shaped caudal (tail) fin steers the fish like a rudder. In front, its upper jaw, which forms into a long bill, cuts a path toward a school of mackerel.

Related to the sailfish and marlin, the swordfish is also a lone, continuous swimmer. It must eat often to support its constant activity. One of the fastest swimmers in the ocean, it can speed up to fifty-five mph (88 kph). Rushing closer to the school, the swordfish folds its pectoral (chest) fins against its body to increase speed. Then the 1000-pound (455-kg) predator charges into the school. Thrashing its head from side to side, it stuns the confused mackerel with its solid sword and eats its fill. In a while the school of mackerel reassemble, and the swordfish glides restlessly off, already preparing for another battle.

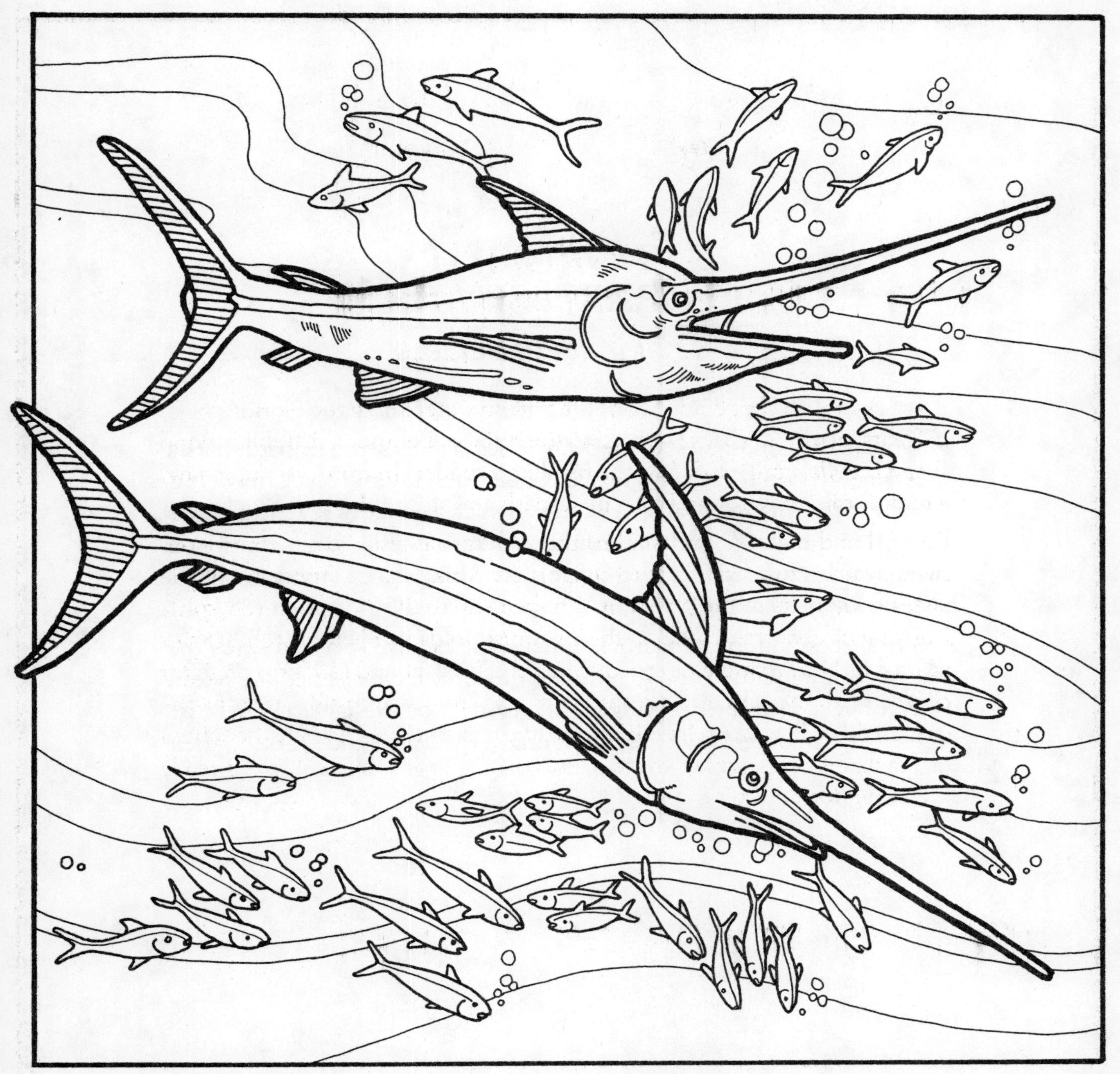

# LEOPARD SHARK

## *Triakis semifasciata*

*Range: Pacific coast* *Length: 7 feet (2.1 m)*

One of the handsomest of the 300 species of sharks, the leopard shark's smooth skin is a silvery green covered with gray and black rings. It is also one of the smallest sharks; females weigh an average of seventy pounds (32 kg), and males about fifty pounds (23 kg). The largest is the whale shark, which grows to fifty feet (15 m) long. Like skates and rays, sharks have no bony skeleton.

A very successful form of marine animal, sharks have survived since the time of the dinosaurs. For 350 million years they have cleaned the ocean waters of sick, dead and decaying sea life. Fairly good eyesight, a keen sense of smell and great sensitivity to vibrations in the water lead sharks to their prey.

# JELLYFISH

## *Pelagia colorata*

*Range: North and South American waters* *Diameter: 2.5 feet (76 cm)*

There are more than 200 kinds of jellyfish and none of them is made of jelly or is really a fish. Jellyfish are invertebrates (having no backbone) with soft, transparent, dome-shaped bodies below which hang long tentacles covered with stinging cells. The body is called a "bell" or "umbrella." The jellyfish moves by contracting and relaxing its bell, like opening and closing an umbrella. Quickly closing the umbrella forces water out from underneath it and pushes the jellyfish in the opposite direction.

Riding through the cool blue sea, the jellyfish trails its tentacles, hoping to sting prey. When it paralyzes the meal, the tentacles bring it up to the jellyfish's mouth, centered on the bell's underside. Almost all jellyfish sting. They can be painful to humans if swum into or stepped on. One little fish, the nomeus, however, is immune to the stinging cells. It fearlessly hides in the jellyfish's tentacles for protection and feeds on its host's leftovers.

# FLYING FISH

## *Oxyporhymphus micro pterus*

*Range: Atlantic and Pacific warm waters* *Length: 18 inches (46 cm)*

The sea offers a number of wonders, but few as delightfully surprising to see as a school of flying fish bursting from the water and sailing into the air. These unique silver and blue creatures, of course, don't actually fly by flapping their wings like a bird does. Instead, they glide over the waves, catching air currents with the large pectoral fins that fan out at right angles from their bodies.

When chased by a predator, such as the dolphin or mackerel, flying fish can leave the water at forty-five mph (72 kph). Soaring fifteen to twenty feet (4.5 to 6 m) over the surface, they travel up to 1000 feet (300 m) before landing back in the sea, tail first. As they splash down, the lower half of their caudal fins starts beating at fifty times a second so that they can pick up speed and take off again if they are still being pursued.

# GREEN SEA TURTLE

## *Chelonia mudas*

*Range: Carribean Sea    Length: 4 feet (1.2 m)*

Sea turtles are one of the few marine reptiles to survive from the Mesozoic era, 190 million years ago, to today. With legs evolved into powerful swimming flippers, sea turtles spend their lives in the water, except when the female lays her eggs.

At night the female green sea turtle crawls onto the same beach where she was born, scoops out a hollow and deposits a hundred eggs into it. After covering them over she returns to the surf, but will come back several times to check on them. In sixty days the eggs hatch. The young tunnel out of the sand, and no matter where they are, head right for the water—even though they have never seen it before! When the turtles are four to six years old *they* will go back to the same beach to start the next generation—if they are lucky. Development of beach property and hunting of these turtles has greatly endangered the ancient creatures' survival.

# GIANT PACIFIC OCTOPUS

## *Octopus dofleini*

*Range: Alaska to Southern California* *Length: 16 feet (5 m)*

The octopus is one of the most highly developed mollusks. Other mollusks include squid, snails and clams. Ranging in size from one inch (.25 m) to this 600-pound (273-kg) giant, they are a favorite food of sharks and seals. An octopus would rather hide than fight. For protection it can squeeze its soft, flexible body into tiny cracks between rocks, as well as change its skin color and texture to blend in with the surroundings. It can also squirt a cloud of "ink" that not only blocks the enemy's sense of smell, but also hides the octopus's escape as it scoots away with its built-in water jet propulsion.

The female octopus takes special care of her eggs by depositing them in the hidden nest she has built. She then cleanses them of fungus and fans the water around them for proper temperature and oxygen, never stopping to eat. The constant activity also helps keep predators away from this fascinating, timid species.

## *CORAL REEF FISH*

# PICASSO FISH

*Rhinecanthus aculeatus*

*Range: Tropical Indo-Pacific waters  Length: 10 inches (25 cm)*

# MOORISH IDOL

*Zanclus cornutus*

*Range: Tropical Indo-Pacific waters  Length: 9 inches (23 cm)*

# LION FISH

*Pterois volitans*

*Range: Tropical Indo-Pacific waters  Length: 12 inches (30.5 cm)*

Absorbing carbonate of lime from the water, small sea animals called coral polyps grow, bud, multiply and die. Over hundreds of years, billions of their tiny limestone skeletons pile up to form reefs. Coral polyps need sunlight, so reefs occur only in shallow, sunlit waters, such as those around the Hawaiian Islands, which host many varieties of beautiful fish.

The brightly marked Picasso fish has a trigger-like dorsal fin that can be raised to wedge the fish into coral crevices, safely away from predators. Equally lovely is the yellow and black Moorish idol, whose long dorsal fin waves gracefully like a royal pennant. Look out for the wildly decorated lion fish, however. Its flashy red and white stripes and feathery collection of fins and spines shout: “Beware! My spikes are poisonous!”

# MANTA RAY

## *Manta birostris*

*Range: Atlantic temperate waters*  *Length: 17 feet (5.2 m)*

Largest of all the rays, mantas measure twenty feet (6 m) from tip to tip across their wide pectoral fins. Because of their broad, flat shape, they take their name from the Spanish word *manta*, meaning blanket or cape. They glide through the sea by flapping these fins up and down. Rays are generally deep water fish, some diving to a depth of 9000 feet (2727 m), but mantas like to cruise near the surface. They can leap fifteen feet (4.5 m) over the water before their 3000 pounds (1364 kg) crash back into the waves.

Also called "devil fish," they have two "horns" above the eyes. The horns are actually another pair of fins which they use to scoop fish, worms and shellfish into their mouths. Mantas are harmless to humans, but their close kin, stingrays, have venomous barbed spines on their tails. Because they live in shallow water, stingrays harm bathers more than any other fish in the sea.

# SEA HORSE

## *Hippocampus hudsonius*

*Range: western Atlantic, New York to Florida* *Length: 5.5 inches (14 cm)*

About fifty varieties of sea horses may be found in most warm sea areas of the world. They are related to pipefish, but their bony plates allow them to swim upright by fanning their rudder-like back fins rapidly—about thirty strokes a second. They use their tails to grasp seaweed for resting or for balancing while chasing after tiny fish and crustaceans to eat. Usually gray to brown in color, sea horses can change color to blend with the background when danger strikes.

The sea horse's oddest feature, however, is that the father gives birth to the young. The female deposits 200 to 300 eggs through a tube into a pouch on the male's front. Here the young sea horses grow for about forty-five days. Then, with a lot of squirming and bucking, the male forces the babies out into the warm salt water. From the moment they are born, the young colts swim freely and independently.

# CALIFORNIA SEA LION

## *Zalophus californianus*

*Range: southwest coast of North America* *Length: 7 feet (2.1 m)*

The performing "seal" that you saw in the circus was probably a female sea lion. They train easily because they are very intelligent, and they *love* the herring with which the trainer rewards them.

You can also see California sea lions in the bays and on the rocks off the Pacific coast. You can hear their "ark ark" barking especially during the summer breeding season when the males fight other males for territory and females birth their pups. Weighing 600 to 800 pounds (273 to 364 kg), males are much larger than the 200-pound (91-kg) females. They also are different from the females in having a higher-domed head.

Masterful swimmers, these cousins of seals and walruses have two pairs of sturdy flippers. With layers of fatty blubber to insulate them from the cold, sea lions are efficient hunters of octopus, squid, rockfish and oceanfuls of herring.

## *TIDE POOL*

## GIANT HERMIT CRAB

*Petro chirus diogenes*

*Range: Southeast Atlantic    Length: 4.74 inches (12 cm)*

## NORTHERN SEA STAR

*Asterias vulgaris*

*Range: Atlantic ocean    Width: 14 inches (35.5 cm)*

## NORTHERN RED ANEMONE

*Tealia crassicornis*

*Range: Atlantic and Pacific oceans    Width: 3 inches (7.6 cm)*

## ATLANTIC ROCK CRAB

*Cancer irroratus*

*Range: Atlantic ocean    Width: 5.25 inches (13 cm)*

Twice a day the ocean waters rise and fall along the shores in an action called the tide. When the water retreats it leaves little pockets of water in the rocks and sand. These pockets are tide pools, which teem with plants, insects and sea creatures.

Colorful, flower-like anemones eat small fish which they sting with their tentacles. Star fish are easy to spot, hanging on to the rocks when the tide goes out. The busy crabs help keep the area clean by feeding on decaying animal matter. See how many creatures you can find on your next visit to the ocean shore.

# SEA OTTER

## *Enhydra lutris*

*Range: North American and Asian Pacific waters* *Length: 5 feet (1.5 m)*

A sunbeam parts the fog off Monterey, California, to awaken a sleeping sea otter. Otters eat, rest, play and sleep in kelp beds offshore—usually on their backs. Rolling out of the seaweed which it wrapped around itself to keep from drifting out to sea, the otter dives for breakfast. Bubbles from air pockets insulating its reddish fur from the chilly waters mark its downward path. Moments later it bobs back with its prizes: a sea urchin and a rock. Floating belly up, the otter smashes the urchin open on the rock and gobbles it down. Whiskers twitching happily, it dives for another. Otters must eat a lot to keep warm.

These friendly marine mammals ranged all along the West Coast, from Canada to Mexico, before they were hunted to near extinction for their rich fur. Only a small band survived on Central California's coast. Now protected, the sea otters' numbers are increasing. Their story is a thoughtful reminder of the delicate balance we must keep with nature.

# MORE FUN BOOKS!

**Collect all four books in the COLORS OF NATURE series!**

Troubador Press Books are available everywhere books are sold, or may be ordered directly from the publisher.

Direct Mail Sales

**TROUBADOR PRESS**
*a subsidiary of*
PRICE STERN SLOAN
360 North La Cienega Boulevard, Los Angeles, CA 90048-1925